Kindergarten Is
COOL!

To Lyra and Avigail, for inspiring this story.
And to Aviya, Baruch, Ezra, Gabriel, Julia Rose, Leah,
Niomi, Noa, and Talia for their inspirations, too.
—Linda ("Nonnie")

Text copyright © 2016 by Linda Elovitz Marshall
Illustration copyright © 2016 by Chris Chatterton

All rights reserved. Published by Scholastic Inc., *Publishers since 1920.* SCHOLASTIC, CARTWHEEL BOOKS,
and associated logos are trademarks and/or registered trademarks of Scholastic Inc.

The publisher does not have any control over and does not assume any responsibility for author or
third-party websites or their content.

No part of this publication may be reproduced, stored in a retrieval system, or transmitted in any
form or by any means, electronic, mechanical, photocopying, recording, or otherwise, without written
permission of the publisher. For information regarding permission, write to Scholastic Inc., Attention:
Permissions Department, 557 Broadway, New York, NY 10012.

This book is a work of fiction. Names, characters, places, and incidents are either the product of the
author's imagination or are used fictitiously, and any resemblance to actual persons, living or dead,
business establishments, events, or locales is entirely coincidental.

Library of Congress Cataloging-in-Publication Data

Marshall, Linda Elovitz, author.
Kindergarten is cool! / by Linda E. Marshall ; illustrated by Chris Chatterton.
pages cm
Summary: Rhyming text describes the activities a child experiences on the first day of kindergarten.
ISBN 978-0-545-65266-7 (hardcover)
1. Kindergarten—Juvenile fiction. 2. First day of school—Juvenile fiction. 3. Stories in rhyme. [1.
Stories in rhyme. 2. Kindergarten—Fiction. 3. First day of school—Fiction.] I. Chatterton, Chris,
illustrator. II. Title. III. Title: Kindergarten is cool.
PZ8.3.M39555Ki 2016
[E]—dc23
2015012510

10 9 8 7 6 5 4 3 2 1   16 17 18 19 20

Printed in Malaysia   108
First edition, July 2016

Book design by Jess Tice-Gilbert

Kindergarten Is COOL!

Written by
Linda Elovitz Marshall

Cartwheel Books
An Imprint of Scholastic Inc.

Illustrated by
Chris Chatterton

When you wake up for school
You'll get dressed really cool,

With your sneakers and socks

And your lunch in a box . . .

Kindergarten's begun.
Big kids *say* that it's fun.
But is that *really* true?
Will it be fun . . . for *you*?

First, you wave bye to home.
Then you're off – on your own!

You're not little, not YOU . . .
You're a BIG kid. It's true!

Go by bus, car, or walk . . .
On the way, there is talk
About new friends and school –
Teachers, pencils, books, rules.

As you enter the door
You see blocks on the floor.

Science stuff to explore,

Spots for "Dress Up" and "Store."

You sing ABCs.
You count 123s.
You count oh-so-high,
It seems numbers fly.

And you *strrrrreeeeeetch* to the stars . . .
Reach to Jupiter, Mars.

Then you rest – very snug –
On the Book Corner rug.
As the teacher reads tales
About singing whales,
Or a duck that's named Ping,
Or the king of wild things.

When your class goes outside,
You jump rope, skip, or slide.

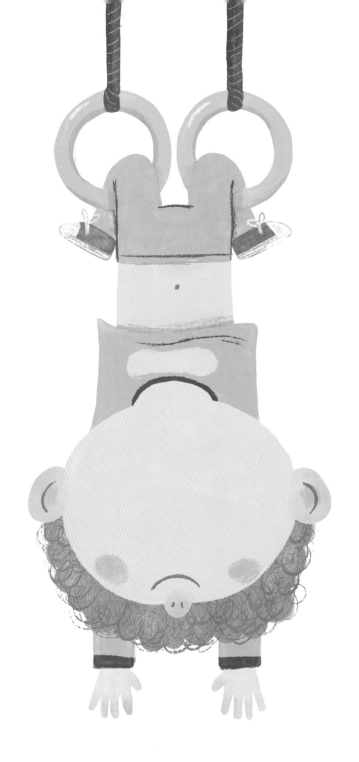

Or you play on the swings,
Monkey bars, or the rings.

By the time recess ends,
You'll have made some new friends.

Then it's time to head back
For your lunch, juice, or snack.

And at playtime, you try,
With a smile and a "Hi!"
To meet the cool girl
With the dark, drooping curl . . .

Or the kid with the smile
That goes on for a mile . . .

Or the boy building blocks,
Who is wearing striped socks.

Will *he* be your friend?
But day's over, and then . . .

 Bb

 Cc

 Dd

"Clean up!" Hurry! Fuss!

Ee

Ff

There's a rush
For the bus!

At night, in your bed,
　　　There is much in your head . . .
About teachers and school,
　　　Music, art, friends, and rules . . .
A whole world to explore:
　　　Science. Reading. And more . . .
Now you're BIG! You're in school!
　　　And . . .
　　　　　It really *is* cool!